Catherine COOK SCHOOL

226 West Schiller Avenue
Chicago, Illinois 60610
312.266.3381
fax 312.266.3616

IN THE MIDDLE OF THE SIXTEENTH
century the first Europeans landed on the island of Kyushu
in the southern part of Japan. Among these fearless sailors,
traders and missionaries that dared sail uncharted seas, was
Francis Xavier of the Jesuit order.

He and the other missionaries had come to preach the
Gospel, but they brought with them a story even older.
Which one of these holy men or adventurers was the first to
tell the tale of Odysseus to the Japanese we shall never know.
But soon the greatest adventure story of our Western culture
was transformed into a native tale.

Odysseus was dressed in a kimono by the Japanese story-
teller, and though he kept his bow, he did not keep his name.
And so the Odyssey became. . . .

THE STORY OF
YURIWAKA

A JAPANESE ODYSSEY

translated
and retold by
Erik and Masako Haugaard
Illustrated by Birgitta Saflund

ROBERTS RINEHART PUBLISHERS

Published by
Roberts Rinehart Publishers
P.O. Box 666 Niwot, Colorado, USA 80544 and
Schull, West Cork, Republic of Ireland

International Standard Book Number 1-879373-02-5

Library of Congress Catalog Card Number 91-65681

Printed and bound in Hong Kong

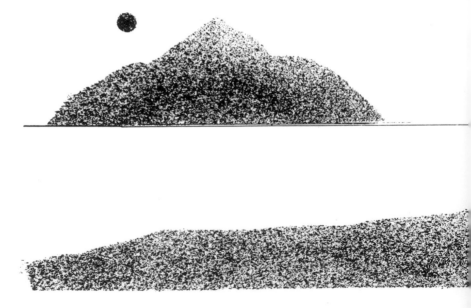

For Chika and Terumi
ECH

For Jack and Jeanne
BS

The tale happened a long time ago. Why, even when your great-great-great-grandfather was in his cradle, the story was already so old that people doubted if it had ever taken place. But that is no reason why one should not believe it, for it may all very well be true.

Far to the south lies the island of Kyushu, surrounded by the blues of water, like a pearl on a piece of blue silk. Anyone who comes from that island will tell you that it is the most beautiful island in all of Japan, and even those who have never visited any other place are sure of it.

But when our story took place, it was not such a happy place to live. Pirates from the country of Shiragi would land on the shores of the island and plunder and murder. These soldiers of fortune cared little whose head they cut off, and their swords were sharp. When the rice was ready for harvesting, the boats from Shiragi would arrive from across the sea and demand the grain. The poor people were so desperate that they sent a message to the Emperor begging him to take pity on them.

At that time the Emperor lived in Nara, and Kyoto was a village that few had heard of. To travel on foot from Kyushu to the Emperor's palace took many weeks. By the time the messenger arrived he looked most of all like a beggar one might throw a copper coin to.

Still the Emperor was gracious enough to allow him an audience in the great hall of his palace. The messenger fell on his knees and kowtowed six times, hitting his head so hard on the floor that the Emperor feared that he might damage it and not be able to remember what he had come for. But he spoke well, and when he described the plight of the poor people everyone cried, and even the Minister of the Right shed two tears, and that no-one had seen before. When he had finished, the messenger kowtowed again and then waited for the Emperor to speak.

YURIWAKA BIDS FAREWELL TO LADY KASUGA AND MIDORIMARU

The Emperor was silent for the very good reason that he did not know what to say. He looked first at the Minister of the Right. His eyes had quickly dried, and he just shook his head. Then the Emperor turned to the Minister of the Left. He had been deeply moved and his cheeks were still wet. He was a native of Kyushu and owned more rice paddies there than you can count before you fall asleep at night. Besides, he was the Minister of the Left, and it is on the left side of the Emperor, as well as on anyone else, that the heart is.

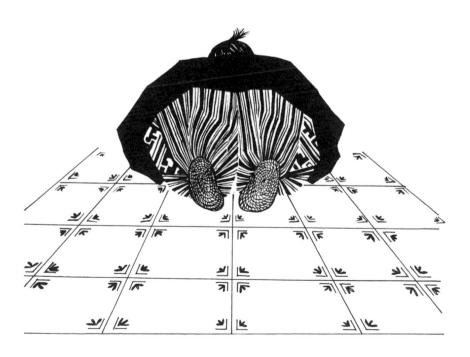

3

"Would it not be wise," he asked, "to send a fleet of ships with soldiers to teach these bandits from Shiragi better manners?"

"Exactly what I have been thinking," said the Emperor, who hadn't been thinking at all.

"My son," the Minister of the Left paused for a moment before he continued, "Yuriwaka, has some ability with a bow and arrow and it is said that even ghosts and demons fear him. If Your Imperial Majesty would lend him three ships I am sure he would acquit himself well."

"Three ships!" the Emperor repeated and glanced at the

Minister of the Right. He came from a country far to the north and did not care much for Kyushu or for the Minister of the Left, so he shook his head once more.

"Your son." The Emperor looked at the Minister of the Left who bowed low and smiled submissively. "Certainly." The Emperor looked straight ahead at the poor messenger who was lying outstretched on the floor as if he had decided to become a rug in the Imperial Palace.

"He shall have the ships," the Emperor declared and with a tiny movement of his hand sent everyone packing so that he could have a cup of tea in peace.

In the district of Bungo on the island of Kyushu stood
the castle of Yuriwaka. He was the strongest man in all of
Japan, if not the whole world. Handsome he was as well
and his wife, Lady Kasuga, loved him to distraction.
Yuriwaka liked to hunt and nothing suited him better than
to wander in the mountains with his favorite hawk,
Midorimaru, on his shoulder and his iron bow in his hand.
No-one but he could bend that bow and seldom did his
arrows miss.

He had just returned from such a hunt when the
Imperial Messenger arrived to acquaint him with the
Emperor's decision.

"His Imperial Majesty has decided to punish and de-
stroy the people of Shiragi who have invaded His sacred
land. In His infinite wisdom He appoints you, Yuriwaka-
sama, to be the instrument of His anger, His righteous arm
that shall avenge the insults to His Honour."

In truth the Emperor had said no such thing, for he was a plain-speaking man and not long-winded. But the Bureau for the Formulating of His Imperial Majesty's Messages could make a no or a yes fill a scroll a mile long. The Emperor had merely said, "Give Yuriwaka the ships and let him be off."

It no doubt was a great honour for Yuriwaka to become commander of the Imperial ships that were to punish the pirates of Shiragi, but his wife, Lady Kasuga, wished that that honour had been bestowed on someone else. She loved her husband and was aware that, though Yuriwaka was strong and his arrows swift, the pirates had bows too and sharp swords. But an order from an Emperor cannot be questioned, only obeyed.

It took some time for the ships to be ready and for Yuriwaka to decide who among his followers were to accompany him. He chose as officers two brothers, Taro and Jiro Beppu, whom he had known since he was a child, and he thought them loyal, for they always praised him whatever he did. But then it is very difficult to distinguish the difference between just compliments and flattery.

Finally the day came when the ships were to sail. All the people of Bungo were down in the harbour to watch their departure and to cheer the brave Yuriwaka and his men. Some of the women whose men were aboard the ship cried but Lady Kasuga did not. Proudly she walked beside her husband, on whose shoulder sat the hawk, Midorimaru. When they came to the ship, Yuriwaka handed the bird to his wife and told him to protect her. The hawk lifted his head and gave a loud cry, as if he had understood his master's command, and jumped onto Lady Kasuga's shoulder.

Lady Kasuga stayed until the mast and sail of her husband's ship had disappeared beneath the horizon, then two tears ran down her cheek as she turned and walked back to the castle. The other women had long ago gone. The one who left first was the one who had cried the most; she declared that evening air was not good for her.

For three long years Yuriwaka fought against the pirates of Shiragi until he had destroyed their boats and conquered their country. But Yuriwaka too had had many losses, and of the three ships that sailed only his own remained. His two officers, Taro and Jiro, were alive but had lost their ships. All victories contain a taste of defeat, and it was certain that there would be homes in Bungo where there would be no rejoicing when Yuriwaka returned. When he had fought the last battle and the last of the pirates had been punished, Yuriwaka declared that now they would return to Bungo. Happily the men hoisted the sails and the wind filled them as they set the course for Kyushu.

One day at sunset the wind dropped and Yuriwaka, who saw an island nearby, declared that they should land there and have a party to celebrate their victory. It was one of the small islands, too tiny for anyone to live on, in the sea of Genkai. Food and wine were brought ashore and a great bonfire lit. Late into the night the men sat drinking sake and staring into the flames, dreaming of their homes.

Yuriwaka thought of the Lady Kasuga and, recalling her beauty, grew melancholy. The men had been singing, and suddenly Yuriwaka wanted to be alone, wanted no other noise but the sound of little waves caressing the sandy shore. He lay down behind a big boulder on the beach, placing his iron bow beside him on the sand. The stars had paled a little as the full moon rose. "Kasuga." He whispered his wife's name and fell asleep.

Soon everyone had followed Yuriwaka into that world where you can see without sight. Only Taro and Jiro were not asleep, nor had they drunk as deeply as the rest.

"The glory will be Yuriwaka's," Taro said and looked out over the sea, "and the shame will be ours for we have lost our ships."

"The Emperor will reward him. He will gain both gold and position and we . . ." Jiro mumbled.

"We will get as much gold as the moon has lent the waves." Taro pointed to the golden reflection which the moon cast upon the sea.

"If only the pirates had killed Yuriwaka." Jiro turned and walked slowly in the direction of where his master slept.

"Then both glory and gold would be ours," Taro whispered as he followed his brother.

"He sleeps and in his dreams he is already in his castle again." Jiro pointed to Yuriwaka.

"This island is a very lonely rock in the sea; only birds visit it," Taro said as he bent down and picked up Yuriwaka's iron bow.

"True. Whoever was left here would need the wings of a bird or the friendship of a dragon to get away." Jiro smiled and the two brothers walked away.

11

When the sun rose Yuriwaka turned in his sleep to protect his eyes from its sharp light. Drowsily his hand
reached for his bow, but it found only sand. With a start
he sat up; the bow was gone. He rose to look for his men,
but the beach was empty and so was the sea. "Taro! Jiro!"
he called. A gull flying above him echoed his screams, but
no-one else answered. "My ship," he muttered, and rub-
bing his eyes, looked at the little bay where last night he
had cast anchor. But there was no ship: the endless ocean
stretched to the horizon.

The little island was like a mountaintop sticking out of
the water. Quickly Yuriwaka climbed it. From its height
he could see the ship; the wind was fair for Kyushu and it
had all sails set. "Traitors!" he shouted as loud as he could,
but only a lizard who was sunning itself on a rock heard
him. Alas, the lizard did not understand him, nor would it
have cared if it did.

Sadly Yuriwaka made his way down to the beach once
more. The fire they had made the night before had gone
out, the ashes were cold. 'Could they not have left me at
least my bow and my arrow,' he thought, 'then I could
have killed a bird.'

The tide was going out
and the stones were filled with mussels. "Kasuga," he whispered his wife's name. He had dreamt of her during the
night and, in his sleep, she had smiled at him so sorrow-
fully as if she knew of his fate.

13

"We did our best to save our master." Taro bowed humbly. "My brother Jiro and I fought like lions, but he was surrounded by our enemies and, when we finally made our way to where he was, he was . . ." Taro paused and then whispered, ". . . dead!"

The Minister of the Left looked at the young man who was kneeling in front of him. His hearing was not so sharp that he could distinguish lies from the truth. "My poor son," he said, "I shall inform the Emperor of what has happened."

"My brother and I are but worthless beings, we should have saved our brave leader." Taro kowtowed four times and then continued, "We thought, out of shame, to end our useless lives. The only reason we decided to spare our insignificant existence was so that we could tell of your son's bravery." Again Taro kowtowed with extreme humility.

"I am sure that both you and your brother did your very best." The Minister of the Left nodded as if he was agreeing with himself. "I shall inform the Emperor of your bravery."

Taro kowtowed once more and then climbed backwards out of the room, making a last kowtow on the threshold.

A worthy young man, the Minister of the Left thought. He appreciated humility in his inferiors.

"Make him and his brother Governors of Bungo," the Emperor declared when he had been told the story of the expedition. The Minister of the Left was not happy about that, for, after all, it had been his son's position. But when the Emperor gave him the title of "Permanent Imperial Privy Councillor" with a pension attached to it, and the right to stand in the presence of the Emperor, he was satisfied as well.

In the meantime Yuriwaka, who had been fond of mussels, had decided that if he was ever rescued he would never eat another one. Each day he climbed to the top of the little mountain and from its summit surveyed the sea. The endless blueness that the wind played upon, sometimes whipping white froth on it, was always the same. Once he spied a boat but it was far away, yet he stayed and followed it with his eyes until it disappeared. That night, because of the boat he had seen, he felt doubly lonely. Some day surely a fisherman will come, he thought,

but, as the days became weeks and weeks months, he felt less sure that he would be rescued. He prayed to all the Gods he knew, and even made a small stone altar and dedicated it to the God Hachiman. But either the God did not hear his prayers or He was too busy to care, for no boat or ship came near the little island. Soon Yuriwaka's fine clothes had become rags. His hair had grown long and a ragged beard appeared on his face. He looked more like a demon to scare children with than the noble youth who had set sail from Kyushu.

In Bungo, the two brothers Beppu had moved into Yuriwaka's castle. The servants did not like them, but Taro and Jiro were the masters, and servants may grumble but they are used to obeying. Their shipmates they had rewarded for betraying their master, and those who were still loyal to Yuriwaka, they had had killed.

Poor Lady Kasuga was kept as if in prison with only one maid to attend her. Some months had gone by when Taro declared that he would marry her. Lady Kasuga said that she would be no-one's wife but Yuriwaka's. She felt sure that her husband was still alive, though Taro and Jiro swore that they had seen him die and had buried him in Shiragi.

"Yuriwaka is my husband and even if he is dead I am still his wife," Lady Kasuga vowed. This did not please Taro; he declared that he was master of Bungo and that everyone, even Lady Kasuga, had to obey him. Lady Kasuga bowed her head and went to her room.

"She is an obstinate woman," Jiro said to Taro.

"If she will not speak to me, then I shall send her to a place where no-one can speak to her," Taro declared and had a prison built wherein he locked poor Lady Kasuga, not even allowing her a servant.

THE BEPPU BROTHERS ABANDON THE
SLEEPING YURIWAKA

On the island her husband became more and more desperate: he thought he would never escape. Each day at noon he climbed to the top of the little mountain, hoping that a ship would be near, and each day he was disappointed. As he sat one day gazing out over endless sea, he noticed a bird flying high up in the sky. 'It is not a seagull,' he thought and rose.

"It is a hawk!" he shouted. "If only it would be my Midorimaru."

The bird circled the island as if it were looking for something; then, as it spotted Yuriwaka, it dived!

"Midorimaru," Yuriwaka whispered and caressed the bird perched on his shoulder. His eyes grew moist, tears ran down his cheeks. The bird looked at its master with eyes of steel, for hawks don't cry.

Yuriwaka's clothes were mere rags. He tore off a little square and then, cutting his arm so that blood flowed, he wrote a letter to his wife on it. He tied the little piece of

linen around the hawk's foot and, lifting the bird on his hand, he said, "Midorimaru, fly home and give this message to Lady Kasuga so that she will know that I am alive."

The hawk looked at its master and then at the sky; though he was tired, he flapped his wings and rose high in

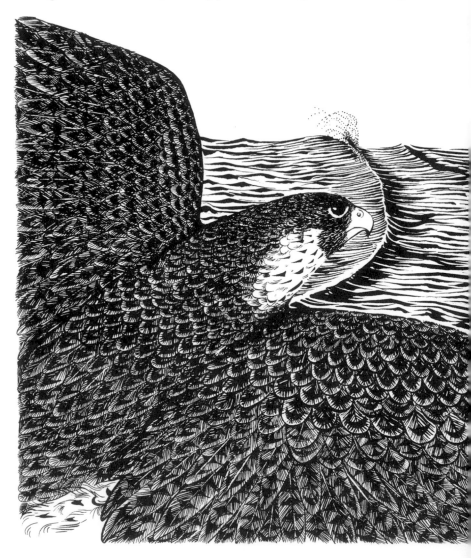

the air. Twice he circled the island before he flew out over the sea towards Kyushu, towards home. Yuriwaka watched until he became a tiny dot in the blueness and disappeared.

Once a week Taro would walk to the prison he had built for Lady Kasuga. He would bring with him a present, sometimes a flower and sometimes a piece of jewelry. When entering the room of Lady Kasuga he would place his gift on the floor in front of her and then demand to marry her. Lady Kasuga would look scornfully at what he had brought and turn her back on him. Though each week saw him equally disappointed, he found the Lady Kasuga more and more beautiful and grew determined to force her to be his wife.

One day after Taro had left, Lady Kasuga stood staring out of the window at the tall wall which had been built around her jail. She looked at the sky and sighed; the little clouds that drifted by were free, but she was not.

"Yuriwaka," she whispered and opened the window. A shadow dropped from the sky and landed on the windowsill. In fear Lady Kasuga stepped back: it was the hawk.

"Midorimaru!" she exclaimed and reached out for the bird. Taking him in her hands, she felt the piece of cloth tied around his leg. Carefully removing it she read its message. "He is alive," she whispered. "He is alive!"

"Midorimaru, come back tomorrow so that you can carry a message to him." Lady Kasuga lifted the bird on her hand and for a moment he looked at her, then flapped his wings and flew away.

When Lady Kasuga realized that her husband had written his message in his own blood, she found the tiniest of inkstones, a brush that fitted it, an inkstick, and a small roll of the finest paper. When Midorimaru returned the next day, she tied all this around his two little legs and ordered him to fly to Yuriwaka.

Bravely the bird rose, his strong wings beating the air. But even though all these writing materials were so tiny and light that one would think they belonged to the smallest of dwarves, to the hawk it was heavy. As Midorimaru made his way out over the sea towards the island, he flew lower and lower until at last his wings almost touched the

tip of the waves. Just as he came near the shore, a wave a little larger than the others reached up and touched the hawk. He tried to rise, but fell into the water and drowned.

When Yuriwaka went down to the beach to gather mussels, he found the dead bird washed up on the sand. He carried the bird to the place he had dedicated to the god Hachiman. He untied the inkstone, brush and paper from his feet; now he could write to his wife, but had no means of sending the letter.

Back in Bungo, his wife sat by the window waiting for the hawk to return. But she waited in vain: the swift wings of Midorimaru would never carry any messages to her again.

One morning Yuriwaka woke by hearing voices. At first he thought he was still dreaming and did not dare to open his eyes for fear of waking. But soon he realized he was not; someone was shouting and not far away. He sat up. It was early morning. The golden ball had just risen from the sea. He ran down to the beach and near the shore he spied a small fishing boat. Yuriwaka shouted as loud as he could while, in excitement, he jumped up and down.

"A demon!" cried one of the fishermen and pointed to the strange apparition who was performing a mad dance on the sand.

"Where there is one, there might be more and some say they can fly through the air. Let us hoist our sail and get away," suggested his partner.

Yuriwaka, who could hear what they were saying, at first did not understand that he was the demon who scared the fishermen. But when he saw that they made ready to sail, he grew desperate. "I am but a shipwrecked sailor from the land of Bungo," he shouted pleadingly.

Now it was lucky that the two fishermen were from the district of Bungo themselves, and when they heard the name of their homeland, they paused. "Who rules Bungo? Who is the Daimio of Bungo?" they asked.

"Yuriwaka," shouted the demon in return.

"That was some time ago," laughed the fishermen. "Yuriwaka is dead. You must have been long on this island."

"It is a year since my hair has been combed or my beard cut. Is Lady Kasuga alive?"

"She is, but is kept in a prison, for she refuses to marry our new master."

"And who is he?" Yuriwaka asked, though he suspected he knew what the answer would be.

"Taro Beppu and his brother, Jiro, rule in Bungo. They were the ones who conquered the people of Shiragi and brought peace to the island of Kyushu."

"Did not Yuriwaka do that?"

"He died in Shiragi. Some say he got an arrow in his back when he ran away," the fishermen laughed.

"Will you take me with you back home? I am no demon. In Bungo I shall reward you."

"We will take you without thought of reward," the fisherman grinned as he looked at Yuriwaka's rags. "I can even lend you some clothes, so you will not have to go naked ashore."

Yuriwaka thanked the two men who drew their boat near the shore to let him climb aboard. He felt it was best not to tell them who he was, but to act the poor ship-wrecked sailor.

"Could you wait one moment?" he begged and ran swiftly to the little shrine he had built. He picked up the inkstone his wife had sent and rushed back to the boat.

"When a man has seen the moon wane and grow full many times on an island like that one," Yuriwaka nodded towards the speck of land which was fast disappearing in the wake, "one would welcome even the company of a demon." He smiled at the two men who had rescued him and they all laughed.

When Yuriwaka finally saw his homeland rising out of the sea, he turned away from his companions so that they should not see his eyes grow moist. But how was he to re-gain his castle? He was weaponless! His two swords he had left on the ship, for he had seen no reason to be armed. He had taken along only his iron bow and that because he never parted with it. Taro Beppu had stolen the bow and Yuriwaka realized that the possession of the bow had made everyone truly believe that he was dead.

It was best, Yuriwaka decided, not to let anyone know that he had returned. He helped the fishermen draw their boat up on the beach and then walked toward the castle that once had been his. He recognised few of the servants; those who had been loyal to him the brothers had got rid of. One of them, who pranced as if he were a peacock just about to unfold his tail, Yuriwaka thought a chief retainer. Humbly he asked if there was work to be had.

"In the stables," the "peacock" sniffed as if he smelt something unpleasant. "That is if you won't frighten the horses."

For several weeks Yuriwaka worked cleaning the stables and doing the most menial work. He found out where his wife was kept a prisoner, but the house was too well guarded. Once when he had ventured near the wall, a soldier had hailed him telling him to go to the cherry orchard and scare the birds away. Truly, Yuriwaka looked more like a scarecrow than a nobleman; he had not cut his hair and beard, and the clothes the fisherman had lent him were little better than rags.

He noticed that a maid brought a tray of food to the prison each evening and he realized that it must be for Lady Kasuga. Once he had tried to talk to the maid but had only frightened her. Secretly he kept watch each evening hoping that somehow he could manage to pass a message to his wife. One day luck smiled on him, for the little maid was late, and in her haste she stumbled and almost fell. He rushed to help her but nothing had happened except that a little porcelain pitcher of sake had fallen over and spilled.

"Please take care that the birds don't get near it while I have the pitcher refilled," the maid asked, being more frightened of being late than of Yuriwaka, and handed him the tray.

On it were many little bowls. Yuriwaka lifted the lids of them all. Into the one which contained the rice he dropped the little inkstone that his wife had sent. Then he replaced the lid and waited for the maid to return.

"If Lady Kasuga should ask you who has held the tray, then tell her it was he of the iron bow," he said as he handed the lacquer tray back to the girl.

The girl did not answer, for she had been scolded by the cook and told that if that happened again she would be

33

demoted to a scullery maid (and they have such awful red hands from scrubbing the big copper pots).

The little maid was still trembling as she placed the tray on the table in front of her mistress. Even prisoners get hungry and Lady Kasuga lifted the lids of the little bowls. When she came to the one that contained the rice, she looked with surprise at the tiny black inkstone perched on top of the white rice.

"Who has touched the food?" she asked.

"No-one!" lied the little maid who was afraid of becoming a little scullery maid with ugly hands.

"Did you see the cook serve it?" Lady Kasuga asked and picked up the tiny inkstone.

"Oh yes, my lady." The girl, who was kneeling beside her mistress, kowtowed once and wished she had never been born.

"Then the cook must have put this inkstone in the rice." Lady Kasuga looked severely at the maid.

"Oh no!" the girl exclaimed, and then realizing what she had said, immediately whispered, "Oh yes," instead.

"What will it be, 'Oh yes' or 'Oh no'?" Lady Kasuga smiled. "It is best that you tell me the truth."

THE ARCHERY CONTEST

"I fell. The sake spilled so I had to run back to the kitchen for more. As the demon was there, I asked him to look after the tray. He must have put it in. I will tell the cook."

"You will not," said Lady Kasuga and put the inkstone into the sleeve of her kimono. "Who is this demon?" she asked.

"He came to Bungo from the sea. The other servants call him the scarecrow. It is only me who calls him the demon, for I am scared of him. His hair is so long and even the nails on his fingers are more like claws."

"Did this demon say anything to you? Or maybe he just spouted fire," Lady Kasuga laughed.

"Oh no, but I am sure he can. He said I was to tell you if you asked that it was 'he of the iron bow'." The little maid, who because of Lady Kasuga's laughter was feeling very safe, snickered.

When the maid had gone, Lady Kasuga took the little inkstone out from the sleeve of her kimono; she looked long at it and sighed.

37

When the cherry trees bloomed, the brothers Beppu decided to hold an archery contest. All the young men in
Bungo practised for weeks beforehand. Some hit the target
all the time and the centre of it some of the time, but there
were others whose arrow fell like lame birds before they
had travelled far. Yuriwaka decided that he too would
enter the competition, but being the lowest of servants he
would not be allowed; besides, he had no weapons.

The competition was to be held in the garden of the temple near the castle. A great crowd of people came to gape and there were little stalls where food and lucky charms were sold. When Yuriwaka arrived, he saw to his surprise his iron bow and quiver containing four arrows lying on a table behind the line where the competitors were to take their stand.

Followed by their attendants, the Beppu brothers arrived. Taro walked a little ahead of Jiro so that nobody should make the mistake of thinking them of equal importance. They seated themselves on a wooden platform which had been covered by a scarlet carpet. Their most trusted attendants and advisors sat behind them in two rows, the most important in the first and the lesser in the last, yet even they were proud of being 'second row' attendants to the brothers Beppu.

"We are holding this competition in honour of Yuriwaka-sama. It is now more than a year since we returned from our great expedition to the land of Shiragi. Our leader ended his noble life there and to his memory I dedicate this contest of skill. His noble bow and quiver of arrows I have had placed on a table. None but he could bend that bow."

Taro Beppu, who had stood up in order to give this speech, seated himself again. He was magnificently dressed and his sword had a silver hilt. Yuriwaka noticed that he had gained weight; he had become fat. The exercise of power does not slim the body, he thought.

Of the first three competitors only one hit the target; when the spectators snickered, their faces grew red with shame. The next lot were better and one even put an arrow close to the centre. Everyone recalled the competitions held when Yuriwaka-sama was alive and how he once had put two arrows in the centre of the target, the second splitting the first one. That was something worth having witnessed—something to tell one's grandchildren.

Yuriwaka had had his hair cut and beard shaved off that morning, but he still wore his old rags and a large hat which hid his features. When the last three competitors had shot their arrows and missed the target more often than they had hit it, he made his way through the crowd. He walked straight to the table where his iron bow lay. As Yuriwaka took the bow and an arrow from the quiver, a rustle went through the people as when the wind suddenly touches leaves of the forest. Straight went the arrow to the very centre of the target, and Yuriwaka smiled. He took a second arrow and drew the bowstring back, and everyone sighed with wonder as the second arrow split the first. Now he took a third arrow and turning towards where the Beppu brothers sat he drew the bowstring taut. Jiro Beppu half-rose as if he were coming forward to greet Yuriwaka when the arrow pierced him. Silently Yuriwaka took the last arrow from the quiver, which now lay empty on the table. Taro Beppu sat perfectly still staring at him, his face was as white as a ghost's. Suddenly he shouted so loudly that all could hear him, "Yuriwaka-sama!" Then he fell forward—the fourth and last arrow had ended his life.

Yuriwaka lowered the bow and took off the broad-brimmed hat and threw it on the ground. Now all could see who he was and loud shouts of "Yuriwaka-sama!" filled the air. The Beppu brothers' attendants kowtowed so furiously that they looked like hungry birds searching for worms. Each of the ones in the first row wished that they had only been second-row attendants and the second-row ones wished that they weren't there at all.

Lady Kasuga was brought from her prison and she and her husband entered their castle once more. A messenger was sent to Nara the very next day, telling the Minister of the Left what had happened. Whether Yuriwaka became Permanent Imperial Privy Councillor like his father I am not sure. Nor do I know what happened to the little maid. Could she have become personal maid to Lady Kasuga? I rather doubt it for she was a silly little thing. I just hope that she did not end up in the scullery among all those big copper pots.

On the island of Genkai I have been told there is a shrine dedicated to Midorimaru. In the Sakuhara Hachi-man Shrine a bow is kept that they claim is Yuriwaka's. But don't you think that such an iron bow would have rusted away long ago?

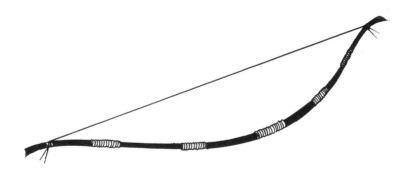

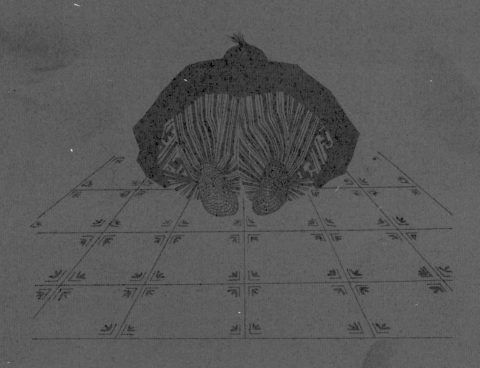